W9-AHH-166

Copyright © 2022 Ji-Li Jiang
Illustrations copyright © 2022 Nadia Hsieh
Cover and internal design by Simon Stahl

All rights reserved. No part of this book may be reproduced in any form or by any electronic or mechanical means including information storage and retrieval systems—except in case of brief quotations embodied in critical articles or reviews—without permission in writing from its publisher, Creston Books, LLC.

Library of Congress Control Number: 2021946705

Published by Creston Books, LLC
www.crestonbooks.co

ISBN 978-1-954354-06-7
Source of Production: 1010 Printing
Printed and bound in China
5 4 3 2 1

To my brother Jason and my sister Jean, for the many times we practiced calligraphy together.
—J.L.J.

To my parents, my sisters, the Huang family, Larry Chen, Asta Wu, instructors and friends who have supported me, and, as always, my agent, Christy Ewers.
—N.H.

Long, long ago, there was no written language in China.
So people drew. They drew the sun and the moon. They
drew mountains and oceans. They drew men and
women. Slowly and gradually, the drawings
became the Chinese written language.
People used brush pens to write, and
they called it Chinese calligraphy.

Eighteen Vats of Water

By Ji-Li Jiang

illustrated by Nadia Hsieh

No one was surprised that Xian loved his brush pen more than any of his other toys. After all, his father was the most famous calligrapher in all of China, and his work was even collected by the Emperor himself.

Xian and his six older brothers all wanted to be great calligraphers, just like their father. They often watched Father dance his brush pen like a graceful dragon, and they too, loved to make their own marks everywhere.

But to formally study calligraphy, Xian had to wait until he turned six. This was the age at which he could be a student of his father.

Patiently and gently, Father showed Xian how to rub the inkstick in circles in the smooth inkstone with a few drops of water to make thick black ink, how to dip the soft brush in the ink evenly, not too much, nor too little, how to hold the brush straight and tight, keeping his elbow raised above the desk, and how to copy each simple stroke.

"Remember," Father said, "to build a good house, you must make a solid foundation. To become a good calligrapher, you must practice the basics first."

Xian was eager to begin. He held the brush straight and tight, keeping his elbow above the table and copied basic strokes — a dot stroke, a vertical stroke, a stroke that curved or waved or twisted into shapes that made him laugh.

Several weeks passed and Xian was getting bored of doing the same thing over and over again. Instead of copying strokes, he sometimes sketched a frog, or inked funny markings on their white cat, or dropped the brush to chase crickets with his friends on the street.

One day, Xian and his friends saw an old woman on the street selling paper fans by their house. She looked tired and sad because no one was buying her wares. When Father noticed her, he took a brush and painted a few words on each fan — words that flew gracefully like

illow branches swaying in the breeze. People swarmed over and
natched up each and every fan within minutes.

urprised and impressed, Xian couldn't wait to become
great calligrapher like his father, loved and admired
y others.

"Father," Xian said. "I have been practicing every day, but it is slow and boring. Isn't there a faster way to become a great calligrapher?"

"Let me tell you a story, son," Father replied. "Once there was a little boy just like you. He wanted to become a master calligrapher, so he practiced every day from sunrise to sunset. In the backyard of his house, there were eighteen large vats of water. After practicing, he always washed the ink from his brush in those vats.

Many years passed, and the water in all eighteen vats turned completely black with ink, and then, only then, did the boy become a good calligrapher."

"You are that boy, aren't you?" Xian's eyes lit up.

Father smiled. "No one can become a great artist without working hard. Ask yourself: what do you really want to be?"

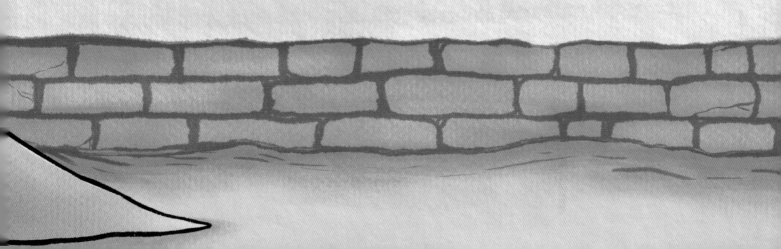

Over the next few days, Xian stared out at the empty backyard again and again, imagining his father as a little boy before he became such a famous calligrapher.

Xian knew what he really wanted to be.

"Father, may I have eighteen water vats?"

Father nodded with a smile.

Soon, the eighteen water vats were hauled in. They were bigger and more beautiful than Xian ever expected. His heart was filled with happiness. The eighteen water vats, shining and shimmering in the sun, would lead him to his dream.

Xian practiced every day. With the vats as a reminder, he worked harder than any of his brothers.

One year passed and the first water vat turned black. Now Xian was advanced enough to copy Father's characters. If he could imitate them well, in several years he would start to develop his own style.

Two years passed and two more water vats turned black.

One morning, one of his brothers said, "I can hardly tell the difference between your imitation and Father's original. Why don't you start developing your own style?"

"True." Xian looked at his calligraphy and thought proudly, "My calligraphy IS as fine as Father's."

The next day he completed a whole page of calligraphy and laid the paper in front of his father.

Father studied the page quietly. Then, without a word, he picked up his brush and added one tiny stroke to one of the characters.

Xian was puzzled. He went to his mother and handed her the page. "Mother, I'm becoming quite skilled, am I not?"

Mother looked at his page for several long minutes. Finally she said, "You have been studying with your father for three years, but there is only one stroke on this page that is as masterful as his."

"Only one?" Xian's eyes widened.

"There." Mother pointed to the very stroke that Father had added. Seeing Xian turn red, Mother said, "To copy the shape of your father's characters is easy, but to grasp the spirit is not. Each of his words has a life of its own."

From that day on, besides painting with his brush, Xian spent hours observing the swans dancing in the pond or the clouds floating in the sky. He was seeking the life of each word he painted.

He worked harder than ever. During the hot summers, he wrapped a dry towel around his wrist so the sweat wouldn't drip on the paper. During the cold winters, he warmed his frozen fingers in hot water and kept on painting.

Many years went by and all the vats were filled with black water. Xian had learned the essence of his father's calligraphy, and more, he had developed his own style. It was called One Stroke Calligraphy, where his painting looked as if it were written with a single stroke — as graceful as swans dancing and as airy as clouds floating.

Just like his father, Xian was now one of the greatest calligraphers in Chinese history. His beautiful work was admired by all and handed down for thousands of years — and with it, the story of the eighteen vats of water.

著名的東晉大書法家王羲之和兒子
被後人稱「二王」。

—379

30

籍琅

（今

史

Author's Note

Thousands of years ago, the Chinese started to develop a written language. Instead of a few dozen letters, they created thousands of characters, and each character was derived from the image of the subject.

The art of Chinese calligraphy developed when the Chinese created brush pens to write the characters with ink. These written characters have evolved over the course of China's five-thousand-year history. A good illustration of this transition can be seen in the change of the character "fish," as shown below.

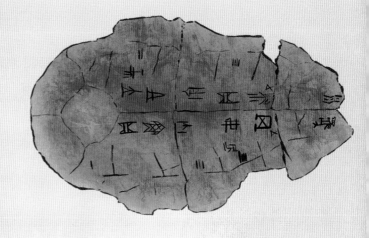

Chinese calligraphy is an art form specific to the Chinese written language. It contains three essential elements — the stroke, the structure, and the spirit.

First: The Beauty of the Stroke
Chinese characters are formed by assembling strokes with a variety of shapes. Using flexible brush pen and ink — the tools of Chinese calligraphy — allows the strokes to be thick or thin, dry or wet, heavy or light, rigid or soft. The various forms of the strokes can be used to express different emotions.

Second: The Beauty of the Structure
Unlike phonetic languages that are based on simple alphabet letters, each Chinese character is composed of multiple parts. The artist's choice of how to position these parts within a character is like an architect designing a building. A good calligrapher will seek symmetry and harmony and use the white blank space to create a balanced structure.

Third: The Beauty of the Spirit
To appreciate this art form, we have to look beyond the individual strokes and characters and focus on the complete image. The "breath" of the whole image — the flow from one stroke to the next, the connection of one character to another, enable the calligrapher to make the whole page come to life. The way the characters relate to each other reveals the calligrapher's emotions to the viewer.

Chinese calligraphy is graceful and expressive, as poetic as a poem, as rhythmic as dancing, and as melodious as music. Picasso once said that if he had started his life as an artist with the knowledge of Chinese calligraphy, he would have been a calligrapher rather than a painter.

Eighteen Vats of Water was inspired by the stories of Wang Xianzhi and his father Wang Xizhi, the distinguished examples of great calligraphers. Although they lived almost two thousand years ago in the fourth century, they are remembered today as the "Two Wangs," and their beautiful work continues to be displayed, admired, and studied in all of China.

Illustrator's Note

When I first read Ji-li's manuscript and was offered the chance to illustrate it, I was excited and couldn't wait to start working on it.

The most interesting and the hardest part was doing the research. I considered what I would be like if I was alive during this period. I thought about what my daily life would be like and what kind of clothing men and women would wear. I imagined what kind of Chinese brush I would use and how I would hold the brush. I found multiple references and discussed them with professors of Chinese literature and history. In my research I found that Xianzhi's father, Xizhi, could hold Chinese brushes in multiple ways. One type is called the "two-finger single hook method." I was surprised to learn that with different styles of calligraphy, there are different ways of holding the brush. With all this complexity, it is understandable why Xizhi is called Shu Sheng, a great calligraphy master.

His son, Xianzhi, had shown an early talent for calligraphy. He started learning with his father as a child, copying his father's style. While learning calligraphy, he realized that talent alone was not enough to become an excellent calligrapher. Rather, this achievement comes through continuous effort and absorbing different life experiences and knowledge.

This book gave me a lot of inspiration as I developed the illustrations. I realized that no matter how talented someone is, dreams cannot come true without hard work. I hope everyone who reads the story can be inspired by the spirit of Xianzhi to keep practicing and working hard on the goals they want to achieve.

About the Authors

Ji-li Jiang is the award-winning author of *Red Scarf Girl*, her middle-grade memoir of life during the Cultural Revolution in China. She has also written several picture books. Ji-li was born in Shanghai, China and now lives in the San Francisco Bay Area. You can see more about her and her work at www.jilijiang.com.

Photo by Hao Wu

Nadia Hsieh received her MFA in Illustration at the Academy of Art University in San Francisco. Nadia's mission is to create characters and stories that focus on empathy and understanding others. She also teaches art education to all ages and can be found playing the piano when she's not drawing. Learn more at www.nadiahsieh.com.